T0380647

PROF. WOBBLE
and the
REVERSAL CAKE MYSTERY

by Karen Peterson

illustrated by Brandon Hayman

To order additional copies of this book, contact:
Xlibris
844-714-8691
www.Xlibris.com
Orders@Xlibris.com

ISBN: Softcover   979-8-3694-2104-8
             EBook   979-8-3694-2105-5

Print information available on the last page

Rev. date: 05/14/2024

With love and appreciation to Dr. James Haden and his awesome staff. Thank you for taking superb care of me...while caring for me! You all are the BEST!

-Karen ♥ Scott

Can you hunt down every slice of the missing reversal cake?

Hidden somewhere in every picture throughout the book is a slice of reversal cake! There are 23 illustrations in all, which mean there are 23 slices of reversal cake, can you find them all? Below are a few hints to help you know what to look for! Good luck!

Chapter 1
Backpack and Butterflies

"Charley…come on, let's go!" This being said in a rather impatient and demanding tone made Charley take notice. He quickly rose and gathered the remaining items to be placed in his superhero backpack, and after a quick inventory check was headed out the door.

Flying down the stairs, he met his sister Lucky's scorching look. She, not one to be late for anything, was standing in the open doorway with her foot tapping impatiently. "Wow Sis give me a break, I had important business to take care of that will hopefully make our day of helping the Professor much easier."

With a roll of her green eyes and a playful push from behind, Lucky directed Charley out into the morning sunshine.

"See, we are right on time after all!" exclaimed Charley, with a smug grin spreading across his freckled face.

Fluttering toward the brother and sister were beautiful butterflies flitting flower to flower. "Get ready, here we goooooooo!" giggled Lucky, looking over her shoulder to see the gloomy look on Charley's face. Knowing all the while he was upset that once again their transportation was gentle and pretty and not rowdy and scary! She knew her brother would much prefer to roar off in a rocket ship or on a charging elephant's back than glide through the sky on a graceful butterfly!

Not as upset as he wanted his sister to believe, Charley did enjoy the ride through beautiful fields, over treetops and gliding toward their assignment for the day.

Chapter 2
Mrs. Teeny Gets a Call

Today was a special day for Charley and Lucky. They were chosen from about a trillion-zillion students to assist their teacher in a top-secret project. And that was an honor in itself! They soon landed in a lovely daisy meadow along the water's edge and were greeted by Professor Wallace Wobble.

Clearing his throat, Professor Wobble suggested they not dilly dally and should get started on their mission.

"What's going on?" inquired Lucky.

The Professor replied, "Our project today is for the locals of Happy Island...a small and cheerful place that only a few are fortunate enough to call home. This paradise offers pink sandy beaches, shells in pearlized pastels, and millions of tall palms that sway in the ocean breeze. Neighbors meet daily at local diners to feast on catch-of-the-day specials and always, ALWAYS finish with desserts that the talented chef has concocted. Desserts are a big thing on Happy Island....and on special occasions, if allowed by watchful-eyed Moms, the entire family orders not one but two yummy, sweet treats."

"Today, my colleagues, is quite an unusual day. For some strange unknown reason, it seems everyone on Happy Island is undoing what they accomplished during the day. We must find the solution to this dilemma. For less is getting done, than would get done, if no one did anything at all!"

With puzzled looks, Lucky and Charley stood patiently by Professor Wobble, observing his wise face for further explanations.

"You see, my young students, we first must get to the bottom of this and detect what exactly has taken place. It seems my secretary, Mrs. Teeny, got an incredibly early morning call of distress from Captain Keeton. His crew aboard the SS Wave Dancer had mistakenly dropped a crate overboard in the rough seas off Happy Island......or **had it been a mistake**?"

Chapter 3
Yummy Cake

"Now what was nestled in the crate is the problem.....delicious lemon-lime, strawberry and chocolate mint Reversal Cakes, which are ALWAYS to be eaten under supervised care of one schooled in "reversal etiquette."   The cakes are so potent, that even the slightest whiff by an unskilled individual would make the whiffer do odd things. For example, doing the opposite of the RIGHT WAY!"

Professor Wobble instructed the kids to collect their backpacks and follow him closely. No dawdling or horseplay would be allowed today since they had plenty to figure out. The inhabitants of Happy Island were relying on them to make things right again. With smiles on their faces and pride in their hearts, Lucky and Charley gave each other a quick thumbs up and scooted to catch the Professor.

Chapter 4
Seahorse Riding

Standing before the three were charming seahorses ready to transport the trio on their mission. Grinning ear to ear, Lucky was quick and jumped on the beautiful lavender seahorse with baseball-sized flowers flowing down her back and tail.....Charley happily hopped on the bright orange ride, leaving Professor Wobble with the apple red steed whose mane was a rainbow of many colors.

Chapter 5
Always Prepared

Ready to begin, Charley and Lucky watched Professor Wobble for clues as to what was expected of them. The students followed his lead and pulled water helmets from their backpacks, while Charley dug deep into his pack and produced a small can with a big fat nozzle under the lid.

Professor Wobble smiled with appreciation at Charley, when he noticed that his pupil had used his head and thought about what supplies might come in handy for the day's mission. Contained in the can was a spray...not just any ordinary household spray, but a rather different and important one. Water Clothes Spray! With one quick spritz, a waterproof coating kept the riders nice and dry during their underwater excursion.

This wonderful invention was discovered out of necessity by Professor Wobble and his students last summer. A very demanding girl, that could swim as well as any dolphin, had signed up for synchronized swimming. Unbeknownst to her what pool water would do to her lovely sunshine yellow hair....what a big surprise she had coming! Every day when the poor classmate emerged from the day's practice, she was sporting a lovely shade of green curls. After testing the spray, her curls were no longer green, but dry and still in perfect yellow pigtails, when coming out of the pool. This made her extremely happy, and her team went on to win the state synchronized swimming championship and no green hair for anyone!

Chapter 6
Underwater Fun

Lucky felt so eager to begin their day's investigation. Charley was right behind her as the threesome dove on their seahorses into the thundering ocean waves and began to submerge in a lovely world of fishes and the unknown.

Using his H2O sound system to speak to Lucky and Charley, Professor Wobble asked the children to keep alert for the lost crate of Reversal Cakes.

Underwater riding happened to be loads of fun! Tiny schools of fish began to follow the happy trio through the ocean depths. The three must have seemed out of place sporting the drab colored water clothes compared to the millions of underwater creatures and their rainbow blasts of scales and shells.

Thinking to herself, Lucky decided to later talk to the Professor about perhaps adding a splash of color to the Water Clothes Spray. Any shade would be delightful, and much more pleasing than the current drab, cheerless one they now wore.

To the children, this project was a fun time, much more enjoyable than a day of school assignments. Who would not love swishing and gliding among the beautiful scenery of the ocean floor while enjoying the ride on gorgeous seahorses!

Chapter 7
Tired Legs and a Big Ol' Cave

Later, the duo began to tire of holding on to the very slanted backs of the seahorses and keeping a constant look-out for clues or perhaps the entire crate of cakes. Even with the saddles, it was hard to look in all directions without slipping off their rides. For neither Charlie nor Lucky wanted to be the one that fell off and give their sibling the chance to poke fun at them.

Eventually, lunch time arrived and Professor announced they would dine as soon as they arrived at the arranged location. Shortly, to the delight and unease of Charley and his grumbling tummy, they rode through the small mouth of a dark scary-looking cave.

But as soon as it was scary, they entered a humongous, brilliant room where they could breathe the refreshing cool cave air. Dismounting and removing their H2O helmets, they thanked the lovely seahorses for the unique jaunt. With a swish of their tails, the trusty mounts scurried off to other escapades as the smiling group waved goodbye.

The cave was lit as if the sun were shining brightly through its water. But after further examination, they discovered the illumination was provided by a million glowing jellyfish bobbing in the shallow cave pond.

Chapter 8
Do Not Touch

Tired of being still so long, Charley was glad to be off his seahorse-pony and, with a boy's curiosity, ran around the cave walks exploring, while Lucky and the Professor unpacked lunches for their dining pleasure.

What a delight to discover that once again Charley had been thinking ahead when Lucky unzipped her brother's pack. Nestled inside were big fat hot dogs with extra mustard and tasty chips that would crunch loud enough to echo throughout the entire cave. This was much more appetizing than the acorns and corn Professor Wobble always served.

On one particularly steep walkway Charley found something very interesting….a tiny bit of what looked like a pink pebble. He stooped over to take a closer look and squealed in surprise. "Hey, look what I found! A tiny smidgeon of Reversal Cake."

"FREEZE!" commanded the Professor. "You must never touch Reversal Cake without proper gear on!"

While saying this, Professor Wobble expertly inserted his hands into heavy-duty lab gloves and then extracted a sealing jar and kitchen tongs from his pack. Using great caution, he lifted the Reversal Cake and safely captured every crumb.

Chapter 9
Lunch on a Turtle

Anxious to feed their rumbling tummies, so they could get started, the three found the perfect place to spread their lunch and quickly began to eat.... all the while watching the cave entrance for their afternoon ride. Lucky inquired about what their next transportation would be. Professor Wobble delightedly said with a gleam in his eyes, "You never know, my dear! Just wait and see."

About that time their table began to ever so slowly teeter and sway side to side. Grabbing their tipping drinks, the kids grinned at one another with knowing looks, as they lifted the tablecloth to peek under. Unbeknownst to them, their dining table was to double as their afternoon ride. Emerging at a snail's pace, a weathered, rumpled, wrinkly smiling face peeked back at them.

"Hello, my old friend, ready to travel?" drawled the ginormous sea turtle. "I have taken the liberty of choosing a deep-sea pod for your transport."

Chapter 10
Pod Riding and Making Faces

All Lucky and Charley could see was what looked to them to be a huge clear egg. Much to their relief they would not have to struggle with seahorse riding all afternoon, since their legs were still tired from their morning travels. To their amazement, the entire top half of the pod began to open and expose rather large seats with plenty of comfortable elbow room for the three of them.

"Please gather your belongings and hop aboard. I promised Mrs. I would be home in time to escort her to the newly opened Seaweed Restaurant tonight, and I do not wish to keep her waiting," explained Monsieur Turtle.

Riding along with plenty of turtle power was terrific. Who would have ever guessed the old fellow had that much get up and goooooooooo!

Charley sat smiling out the window with searching eyes for a clue to the Reversal Cake mystery. Zipping past large schools of fish and watching a funny little fairy-like creature appear, smile, make faces, and disappear almost as quickly as she materialized. Charley blinked, then rubbed his eyes, surely, he was just sleepy after his good lunch and kept dreaming of the little creature outside his window.

Chapter 11
S.S. Wavedancer and Sticky Feet

Captain Keeton's crew had endured a very busy and tiring workday aboard the SS Wave Dancer making scheduled stops among the tiny islands delivering much needed supplies for grocers, restaurants, and fast-food places. Delivery days keep Captain Keeton and his crew of six extremely busy every Monday through Wednesday and the remainder of the week wasn't much easier. That's when the SS Wave Dancer is rented for fishing expeditions and whale watching parties…and this time of the year is booked solid.

After charting their way through dangerous waters around the grouping of islands and just about ready to turn in for some much-needed rest, whacky mesmerizing music began to play… instantly engulfing the entire vessel. Immediately, water began to spray over the ship's bough.

Fearing the Wave Dancer had sprung a leak, the crew ran to investigate. Slipping and sliding in water that now had a faint blue glow and immediately making the deck sticky and difficult to move their bare feet. The crew was unsure what to make of it. Suddenly, the bluish water was thicker with wiggles, bounces, and jiggles. Now standing in knee-deep dessert, the crew scratched their heads and exchanged worried looks. Perhaps they should wake the Captain for his wise commands!

Chapter 12
Blue Lips, Water Sprite, and a Crate

One curious mate stooped and scooped a handful of the shaky blue stuff and was pleasantly surprised after tasting the delicious snack. He exclaimed, "Yum! This is great!"

His fellow workers followed his lead and soon no trace of anything out of the ordinary was left….that is, except the silly music and the shipmates' blue lips and hands. Instantly, the mesmerizing tune's volume turned low. On the ship's rail sat a very lovely Water Sprite, draped in fairy-like clothing that shimmered and shone in the moonlight. "Good evening my fine gents," sang Peaches with a mysterious grin on her lovely little face.

Little did the crew know they had just fallen for the first of many tricks that Peaches had up her sleeve.

It's a little-known fact that Sprites LOVE Reversal Cake, especially for their birthdays....and Peaches' friend, Pearl, was celebrating her 203rd birthday today. This would make a wonderful gift for the surprise party in the Coral Gardens, below the SS Wave Dancer. Most Sprite parties were rather boring, since it was hard to get your hands on any cake there in the ocean....much less a Reversal Cake!

Now that the witty Sprite had the attention of Captain Keeton's deck hands, she proceeded to sing instructions in her teeny tiny Sprite voice. "Gentlemen, with caution as to not damage the crate, please help me cover it in this delightful birthday wrap, so Pearl won't see what her gift is and spoil the surprise."

The crew gathered and with swift hands followed instructions. Skillfully wrapping the crate in cheerful colors and a big purple bow. "Lovely, just lovely!" sang Peaches, with a happy grin spreading across her tiny little Sprite face.

"Now my friends, please lift the crate ever so gently and let it fall into the net beside your boat. Careful, so as not to crumble the cakes!"

Without so much as a question, the crew complied. Over the rail's edge the crate toppled, making a soft splash. "And remember my blue-lipped sailors.... not a word of this to anyone. Thank you, fellows, and nighty-night!"

In the blink of an eye Peaches sprang overboard following the crate as the music came to an abrupt halt. The only sound were waves lapping against the boat sides and Captain Keeton's snoring.

Eyeing the crate and knowing she should not, Peaches sneakily unwrapped one end of the gift and pulled out a small Reversal Cake. One taste is all she wanted! Unfortunately, she never got the opportunity. With cake in hand, Peaches tried to sit on a bench, but much to her dismay, as soon as she sat, the bench flipped her through the water, causing the cake to explode into a million crumbs, dispersing as if blasted from a cannon.

Chapter 13
Follow That Sprite!

Back in the sea-pod, Lucky giggled and professor Wobble inquired, "What tickled your funny bone?"

Unsure what really had, since she normally was labeled the more serious of the two siblings, Lucky, quieting another snicker, explained, "A little water creature keeps making funny faces and sticking her tongue out at me. See, there she is again!" As she said this, the comical Sprite, Peaches rushed past the water egg leaving trails of popping bubbles in her wake. "Oh wow," exclaimed Charley, "I wasn't dreaming her! She is real!"

"For goodness sakes!" exclaims Professor. "That is a Sprite, and they love to play tricks and jokes on the unsuspecting. We shall follow as close as possible, but a distance must be kept between us, so as not to fall under her musical spell and be her next victim. QUICKLY, put your aquatic hearing silencers on and adjust to quad 5, so we can communicate with each other safely. These Sprites are clever creatures and can cast their unwanted spell before you can blink an eye. Be cautious and keep scanning the area for Reversal Cakes or naughty Sprites, who I am sure have played a big part in this mystery."

Chapter 14
Party Plans

Down in the coral gardens, all had been arranged for Pearl's surprise party. Everyone in the Sprite village had done very well keeping the party a secret. Although, this must have been difficult for some of the Sprites, because, as much as playing pranks, they loved to talk.

Gem-filled oysters lined the path to the birthday party site and schools of neon fish darted in unison to illuminate the waters overhead, creating an amazing rainbow effect.

The main village was decorated with millions of miniature balloon fish in pastel hues floating above each table. Starfish of all sizes and colors attached to the sea reeds and ocean grasses mimicking the stars in the sky, high above the ocean floor. Tables overflowing with gifts and tasty treats awaited the unsuspecting Pearl and many, many anxious guests. This was going to be a special day to celebrate everyone's beloved Pearl.

Entertainment had been an easy task, with Pearl's singing society sisters, The Centennial Sprites, insisting on presenting a sing-along and possibly sharing a few show tunes that Pearl loved. Party decorations were perfect as all the entertainers and guests gathered to wait in anticipation of the Birthday Sprites arrival.

"Where is she? I knew something like this would happen with Peaches if I did not keep an eye on her this afternoon. Even after promising she'd be early for the celebration, she does tend to lose track of time when out for a swim or chatting with neighbors," whined the matron Sprite, Goldie .

" In fact, just last week she forgot to watch the timer as she was giving me a facial and left the algae mask on twice as long as clearly instructed. My beautiful complexion still has a tint of green on my cheeks and chin. Or the incident where she was baking cakes for the community fair and began picking and arranging sea bonnets for the tables, and after six hours remembered to take the cakes out of the oven, or should I say charcoal dust! Thank goodness she was quick on her feet

and raced to the Saltwater Diner and bought all their pies and cakes, for it's not a fair without glorious sweets! I suppose she just gets involved with being Peaches or whatever she's doing and sometimes loses track of time occasionally."

On the edge of the Coral Gardens, knowing the egg pod and its passengers were in hot pursuit, Peaches performed, as she loved being the center of attention. Zigzagging and cannon balling straight up to the surface and plunging back through the water's depths. With the graceful moves of a ballerina a tenth her age. She took the curious trio on a fascinating and colorful excursion. Touring lovely coral beds full of barnacles, shrimp, crustaceans, and other aquatic life, and through treacherous shark infested waters that only silly-willies or the very brave dared to venture.

Very impressive that the trio's faithful turtle comrade was so agile and mobile enough to stay glued to the Sprites' wake. He matched her every swerve, plunge, and loop-to-loop with almost as much finesse as she.

Chapter 15
Undoing What's Done

However, the inhabitants of Happy Island were having quite a difficult day. Ever since Monday's sunset, odd incidents had been occurring all over town.

Very proud of the excellent job of vacuuming the floors and seats in their new car, Clover, Hal and their twins Rusty and Rowdy decided to go to the beach for an evening swim. After 30 seconds of water play, the family began to feel a little peculiar and decided to go home for dinner. Instead of toweling off and slipping on their flip flops before sitting in the brand new car....they all plopped soggy behinds down, scattering salty wet sand and shells everywhere. Hal then proceeded to drive out the entrance gate, passing the guard, with everyone waving but not being seen since Wally was busy erasing the words in his crossword puzzle book that he had just proudly completed.

Across town Mayor Cypress docked his little fishing boat and accidentally dropped the dip net overboard, he unceremoniously scooped the net up, wiped his moist hands on his favorite fishing shirt and returned to the office.

Upon entering, Mayor Cypress used his pink eraser to remove his name off all the day's documents he had so diligently read and signed......papers that approved the new swing set at the park, okayed the yearly dog show to have their Bark & Howl parade around the town square and lastly give funds to be spent for new flower gardens in front of Sugar & Cream Coffee Shop. ALL reversed and undone!

After an evening stroll collecting colorful oddly shaped shells, Jasper felt a bit strange. He did not have a clue as to what the issue might be. An overwhelming urge made him return to the building site where he had labored all day. Jasper unnailed every nail he had proudly hammered into the wood and returned them to their boxes. Thus, following his day's work, he had reversed everything he had worked so hard on completing.

Other locals were confused when they also began to reverse their day's activities. It was catching! Everyone on Happy Island had caught it and didn't even know they had!

Chapter 16
Tardy Peaches

"Jeepers!" said Peaches, as suddenly her brain kicked in. She was to have met Goldie in the Coral Gardens for an afternoon of celebrating Pearl with yummy lip-smacking treats and birthday gifts. Goldie was her next-door neighbor and a delight to be with. How could she be so unthinking to keep sweet Goldie waiting!

With her mind on sweets, Peaches was over teasing the sea-pod full of strangers and decided to turn into the next jumbo-sized conch shell and lose them. Then she could circle back to join her understanding friend when they whizzed past.

Little did Peaches realize the watchful eyes of Charley and Lucky had already noticed the entire village of Sprites. The party goers were busily trying to rewrap the ends of a crate that clearly was marked Reversal Cakes.

Immediately, the intelligent turtle understood what his commuters had spied and continued following Peaches. Although not as close, so as to appear she had lost them after hiding in the conch shell. They circled wide and returned to the spot where all the hidden gaiety was about to take place and watched. Professor Wobble, Charley and Lucky needed to put their heads together and come up with a solid plan as to the retrieval of the lost crate.

Counting to thirty after the tailgaters had passed, Peaches smoothed her hair, straightened her outfit, and took off to meet Goldie. Arriving at the Coral Gardens in record time, so as not to be extra tardy, Peaches spied Goldie sitting with her back to the entrance. When suddenly a huge "SURPRISE" was shouted from all directions for the Birthday Sprite Pearl.

By the time Pearl's heart finally quit thumping so fast, she was overwhelmed with love for all her friends, and the fact that her heart was..... still ticking....... for today was her birthday and she was happy.

The entire village had shown up to celebrate Pearl. Hugs and kisses were showered upon the little spry Sprite from neighbors of all ages. Immediately, the party was in full force. Food, drink, music, and lots and lots of laughter.

Pearl was particularly interested in the huge gift table and what the brightly wrapped packages might be hiding inside. It took Pearl quite some time to tear open and examine all her special gifts. She opened pearls for her hair, a dance lessons certificate, an all-expense paid trip to the Great Barrier Reef and many many other thoughtful and welcomed surprises.

And then there stood Peaches smiling right into Pearl's face, with the knowing look that her gift was the best of all! Unwrapping with the speed of a race car driver, Pearl let out a squeal of delight when in her lap was not one, not two, but an entire crate of Reversal Cakes in her absolute favorite flavors.

"Thank you, thank you, Peaches! Let's all enjoy a big fat piece of cake!"
During the afternoon entertainment, the entire group of partygoers eagerly pigged-out on mammoth platefuls of lemon-lime, chocolate mint, and strawberry Reversal Cake.

"Professor, we're too late!" said a very distraught Lucky, watching a happy Sprite help others to seconds of cake. "The cakes have been cut and almost all eaten.... now what?"

"Don't fret…all is not lost. We shall follow through with our plan and still help the locals of Happy Island before dinnertime."

The trio watched the festivities from a bird's eye view, well hidden in the sea reeds and grasses, from a ledge high above the Sprite Village.

Chapter 17
A Hard Day

Meanwhile, Happy Island residents, experiencing a difficult day of undoing, were gathered at Town Hall, and trying their best to not undo anything else. At this rate, the town would soon fall apart in one way or another, from all the unsigned laws, unnailed nails and undoing things done. No one was certain how help would come…. but it better get there fast!

Chapter 18
Old Friends Meet Again

While the party was in full swing, no one noticed Goldie's absence as she went to investigate the strangers watching from afar.

Charley and Lucky could not believe their eyes, for swimming directly toward the pod was the most beautiful and regal looking Sprite in the entire Sprite world. Professor Wobble instructed the children to lower their aquatic hearing silencers to level 4, until he was sure what the Matron Sprite had in mind. Not knowing if she came as a friend or ready to play Sprite games with them.

"Why it is my old acquaintance, Professor Wallace Wobble! How have you been my friend?" asked Goldie with a guilty look…. knowing all the while why the Professor, Charley and Lucky were there watching the party.

Realizing she came with no pranks to play; Professor Wobble motioned for the children to remove their silencers and meet Goldie. It took a short conversation before the Professor and kids were promised that the wrong would be righted, Immediately!

With a swish, all that was left was sand-clouded water and sea fans swaying in the wake, as Goldie hurried to rejoin the merriment in the gardens.

Chapter 19
Thanks for the Ride

Checking his timepiece after waking from a short afternoon nap, Monsieur Turtle checked on his riders and was given a happy nod by the Professor, signaling it was time to head home.

"How, who, when?" was all Charley could say.

"We will just have to wait and see at this point," confided Professor Wobble, as he began to pour a nice cup of strained lima bean juice for his fellow travelers. Quickly, Charley opened his pack and withdrew Lucky and himself an apple juice instead. No more lima bean juice for them!

The return trip zoomed by for Lucky and Charley…both pleased with the outcome of finding the source of Happy Islands problem and hoping even more it was righted. Only time would tell now.

Waving goodbye and calling "Thank You" to Monsieur Turtle as he expertly dove into the crashing waves, the trio gathered their belongings and waited for their final ride of the day.

Chapter 20
Rescuing Happy Island/Problem Solvers

Back in the Coral Gardens, with full tummies, hours of party details to gossip about for weeks to come, and to-go boxes of late-night snacks, including Reversal Cake, Pearl's celebration came to a close. Before Goldie said her final farewell, just one detail regarding Peaches was left to be tended to.

Trying to stay on the other side of the sea reeds during the entire party, Peaches knew what was coming and dreaded it, but didn't care, since her gift to Pearl was still the best anyone had given the loveable birthday Sprite!

"What an utterly fantastic day this has been with everyone at Pearl's party," said Goldie, as Peaches tried to keep her head low and sneak out behind the big clam shells.

"Ah, what…? Oh yes, it was quite lovely and loads of fun…. Well, I must be zipping along…..Things to do, places to be," muttered Peaches. All the while knowing she should be still and have her talk with Goldie, she knew it was coming. Better to face her and get it over with.

"Okay, I know it wasn't right for me to take the Reversal Cakes, but I know Pearl absolutely adores them. And I did give the deck hands on the SS Wave Dancer some lovely blue jiggly stuff in exchange," whined Peaches with a teeny tiny tear welling in her eye.

"That, my dear, isn't the true problem. I understand through the aquatic grapevine that Reversal Cake mist has been blowing over Happy Island and that is not a good thing for us to let happen. The Water Sprite Society has taken an oath to protect and never misuse our power over Happy Island residents or sailors on the high seas. I thought we all understood the power of Reversal Cake! People are never able to resist the REVERSAL part of the cakes and that causes many problems and troubles they must deal with."

"What shall we do to make this right for the locals of Happy Island?" inquired Peaches with concern.

"There is only one choice we must consider."

With no further words being spoken, Peaches looked into Goldie's sensible eyes and nodded. Immediately, she disappeared around the sea reeds and collected the now empty Reversal Cake crate, calling out to the lingering guests that she needed assistance. In unison, all agreed to help and stood before Peaches and Goldie while information was formed, and plans were planned.

When a Sprite decides to accomplish a task, it gets done quickly and efficiently. Peaches explained to the party goers what had taken place, and everyone scattered. Within minutes, all had gathered with items in hand, ready to start the Reversal of the Reversal Cake effect on Happy Island and its inhabitants.

One by one the Sprite villagers placed their bits and pieces into the Reversal Cake crate and Peaches closed the lid.

Goldie stepped forward and raised her hands to quiet the crowd. "All is prepared and ready to take place when the sun touches the western horizon in its evening decline."

When the exact moment of sunset arrived, schools of fishes began to swim in small baby circles, others in larger oblong circles, and still others in great big whale sized circles….faster and faster…churning the water into a tornado funnel that reached from ocean floor to the ocean waves. At the precise moment that the rotating water was perfect, Peaches opened the Reversal Cake crate and set free the contents.

Immediately, in faultless unison, the swirling fish reversed direction, sweeping the Reversal Cake crate into the vortex, and elevating it to the water's surface, correcting Peaches' unthinking ways.

Chapter 21
Happy Island Happy Again

Dawn broke on a cloudless, sunshiny day. Swaying trees filled with chirping birds, with all the plants and houses of Happy Island cradled in heavy salty dew. No one the wiser, no one caring about yesterday's craziness and upsets. Just the excitement of a beautiful day to enjoy while at work, play, or sampling delicious ooey gooey desserts, making sure that lots gets done on this perfect day and last, but not least, STAYED THAT WAY!

The End

Printed in the United States
by Baker & Taylor Publisher Services